To Adam,
S.McB.

For Di,
A.J.

First published 2007 by Walker Books Ltd
87 Vauxhall Walk, London SE11 5HJ

10 9 8 7 6 5 4 3 2 1

Text © 2007 Sam McBratney
Illustrations © 2007 Anita Jeram

Guess How Much I Love You™ is a registered
trademark of Walker Books Ltd, London

The right of Sam McBratney and Anita Jeram to be
identified as author and illustrator respectively of this
work has been asserted by them in accordance with
the Copyright, Designs and Patents Act 1988

This book has been typeset in Cochin

Printed and bound in China

British Library Cataloguing in
Publication Data: a catalogue record
for this book is available from the
British Library

ISBN 978-1-4063-0452-7

www.walkerbooks.co.uk

GUESS HOW MUCH
I LOVE YOU
—— *in the* ——
SPRING

Written by
Sam McBratney

Illustrated by
Anita Jeram

WALKER BOOKS
AND SUBSIDIARIES
LONDON • BOSTON • SYDNEY • AUCKLAND

Little Nutbrown Hare
and Big Nutbrown Hare went
hopping in the spring.

Spring is when things start
growing after winter.

They saw a tiny acorn growing.

"Someday it will be a tree,"
said Big Nutbrown Hare.

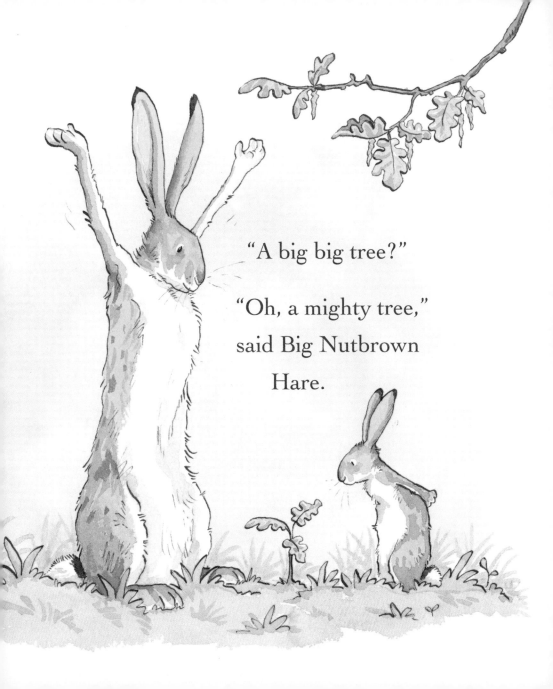

"A big big tree?"

"Oh, a mighty tree,"
said Big Nutbrown
Hare.

Little Nutbrown Hare spotted a tadpole
in a pool. It was a tiny tadpole,
as wriggly as
could be.

"It will grow up to be a frog,"
said Big Nutbrown Hare.

"Like that frog over there?"

"Just the same as that one,"
said Big Nutbrown Hare.

A hairy caterpillar slowly crossed the
path in front of them, in search of
something green to eat.

"One day soon it will change
into a butterfly," said
Big Nutbrown Hare.

"With wings?"

"Oh, lovely wings," said
Big Nutbrown Hare.

And then they found a bird's nest among the rushes. It was full of eggs.

"What does an egg turn into?" asked Little Nutbrown Hare.

"A bird."

"A big big bird?"

"Well ... a grown-up bird,"
said Big Nutbrown Hare.

Does nothing stay the
same? thought Little
Nutbrown Hare.
Does everything change?

Then he began
to laugh.

"What does a little
brown hare like
me turn into?"
he said.

Big Nutbrown Hare
 began to think,

and think...

Goodness me, did he
know the answer?

Yes!

"A Big Nutbrown Hare — like me!"